Words to Know Before You Read

climb

high

ladder

pool

summer

swim

www.rourkepublishing.com

Edited by Luana K. Mitten
Illustrated by Anita DuFalla
Art Direction and Page Layout by Renee Brady

Library of Congress Cataloging-in-Publication Data

Greve, Meg
 Swim for It / Meg Greve.
    p. cm. -- (Little Birdie Books)
 ISBN 978-1-61741-805-1 (hard cover) (alk. paper)
 ISBN 978-1-61236-009-6 (soft cover)
 Library of Congress Control Number: 2011924657

Rourke Publishing
Printed in the United States of America, North Mankato, Minnesota
060711
060711CL

www.rourkepublishing.com - rourke@rourkepublishing.com
Post Office Box 643328 Vero Beach, Florida 32964

Swim for It!

By Meg Greve

Illustrated by Anita DuFalla

4

On a hot summer day, elephant and his friends go to the pool for a swim.

POOL →

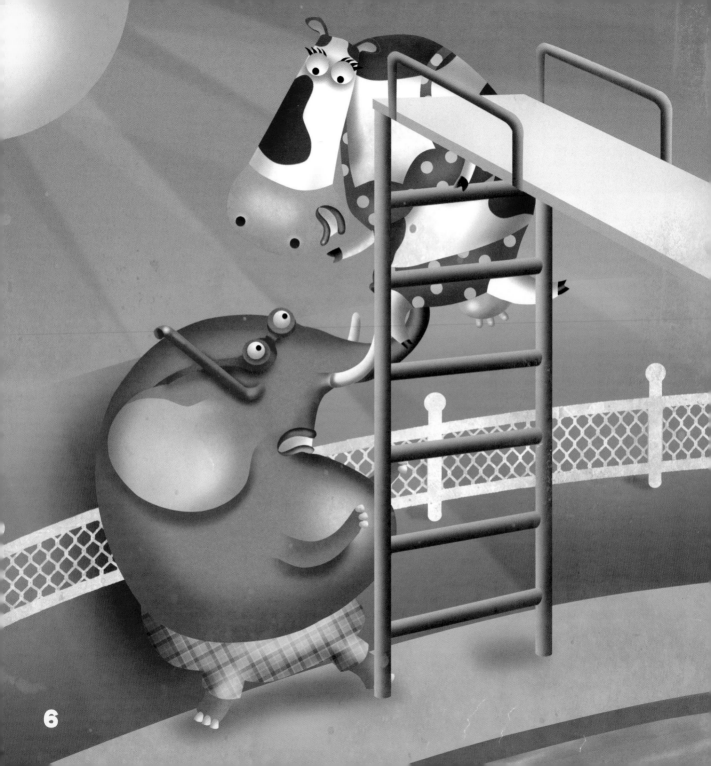

6

Pig climbs a tall, tall ladder to the top of a high dive.

He jumps in the pool and yells, "Jump, cow, jump!" Cow jumps in.

9

Pig and cow yell,
"Jump, elephant, jump!"

11

Elephant climbs up to the very tippy top.

13

14

Elephant climbs down.
"Jump, elephant, jump!"

15

16

Elephant climbs up to the very tippy top.

He closes his eyes, holds his trunk, and JUMPS!

SPLASH!

18

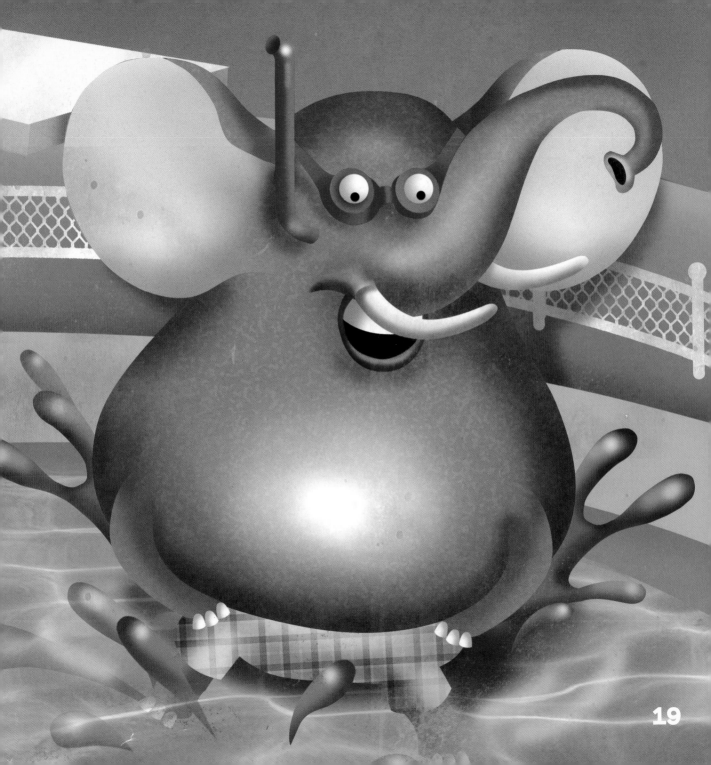

19

"Let's go find another pool."

20

POOL

21

After Reading Activities

You and the Story...

Who was scared to jump off the diving board?

Have you ever been scared to do something?

Why do you think they needed to find another pool at the end of the story?

Draw a picture of a time you were scared.

Words You Know Now...

Each word is missing letters. Can you write the words on a piece of paper and fill in the missing letters?

_ _ imb

hi _ _

ladd _ _

p _ _ l

summ _ _

_ _ im

You Could...Plan a Pool Party

- Use a calendar to find out what day you would like to have your party.

- Make invitations inviting your friends to come to your party. Make sure the invitations tell:
    - What the party is for
    - What your guests need to bring (bathing suit, towel, change of clothes)
    - The date and time of the party
    - The place where the party will be

- Plan what you will do at the party.
    - Will you play pool games?
    - Is there a song you could sing at the party?

- Make a list of what supplies you need for the party.

About the Author

Meg Greve lives in Chicago with her husband, son, and daughter. Both of her children love to swim and jump off the high dive!

About the Illustrator

Acclaimed for its versatility in style, Anita DuFalla's work has appeared in many educational books, newspaper articles, and business advertisements and on numerous posters, book and magazine covers, and even giftwraps. Anita's passion for pattern is evident in both her artwork and her collection of 400 patterned tights. She lives in the Friendship neighborhood of Pittsburgh, Pennsylvania with her son, Lucas.